NEVER BRUSH A BEAR

For Harriet,
love from Dad-dad.
– S. H.

Huge thanks to Emily Talbot
at United Agents, and to
Rhiannon, Emily, Sarah, Malena
and the Happy Yak team for
helping bring Herschel to life!

Brimming with creative inspiration, how-to
projects, and useful information to enrich your
everyday life, quarto.com is a favorite destination
for those pursuing their interests and passions.

The Quarto Group
Inspiring | Educating | Creating | Entertaining

© 2022 Quarto Publishing plc
Text and illustrations © 2022 Sam Hearn

Sam Hearn has asserted his right to be identified as the author and illustrator of this work.

First published in 2022 by Happy Yak, an imprint of The Quarto Group.
The Old Brewery, 6 Blundell Street, London N7 9BH, United Kingdom.
T (0)20 7700 6700 F (0)20 7700 8066
www.quarto.com

A catalogue record for this book is available from the British Library.

ISBN: 978 0 7112 6552 3

9 8 7 6 5 4 3 2 1

Manufactured in Guangdong, China TT032022

FSC
www.fsc.org
MIX
Paper from
responsible sources
FSC® C016973

Here we have Herschel – he likes to brush hair.
Head stylist, pet pamperer extraordinaire!

He dreams of awards,
and longs to win prizes,
For coiffuring creatures
of all shapes and sizes!

Like beagles!

Or bunnies!

Or ponies!

Or pugs!

*(He'll even brush fir trees
and Grandma's best rug.)*

Whatever your pet is, he'll brush it with care...

What?! Did you just say

BEAR?

A bear's not a pet!
And brushing one is something
you need to forget!

Oh Herschel!
Come on now –
You just wouldn't **dare!**
I seriously think you should...

NEVER brush a BEAR!

BEARS THIS WAY

First of all, Herschel, they live miles away!
To find one, you'll have to go hiking all day.

You'll have to
climb mountains...

then trek through
the woods...

You haven't turned back yet?
Well maybe you should!

You want to keep going?
OK, fair enough.
I see you're determined,
but what about tough?

If you want to brush bears
then you'll need to be brave,
For a bear always knows when
you're outside its cave...

You'll hear a low growl,
sniff a whiff in the air...

Oh crikey! You've found us a

GREAT BIG WILD BEAR!

Hold on a minute – something's not right!
This bear isn't wild...
He seems quite polite?

In fact, he looks friendly! And really not shy...
Go on then, Herschel. Give brushing a try!

Brush his arms first – though this might be tricky,
Bear fur is tangly and really quite sticky!

And now, brush his chin,
which he seems to quite like!

Watch out round
his mouth, though –
bear teeth are
like spikes!

Next, brush his legs – but go slowly, OK?
Just brush all the mud and pine needles away.

So far, so good – now move round to his belly,
(I warn you though, Herschel, this bit could be smelly!)

Now brush his head –
it will be quite a test,
Oh! That's surprising,
he likes this bit best!

But here's what's important – there's really no doubt,
When a bear lifts his arms up, you'll need to watch out!

One hair out of place
could end in a pickle,
'Cause hairbrush plus
bear armpit equals...

...A TICKLE!

See, now you've done it – the brush has gone flying!
You'll roll down the hill, laughing so much you're crying!

That tickle has sent you downhill in a blur,
A bundle of bushy-brown-leafy-twigged fur...

... and you'll land on your bum,
in a big squelchy puddle.

Just look at that bear –
what a big hairy muddle!

Never mind, Herschel,
things go wrong
now and then...

... you'll just have to brush him all over again!